W9-BMQ-188

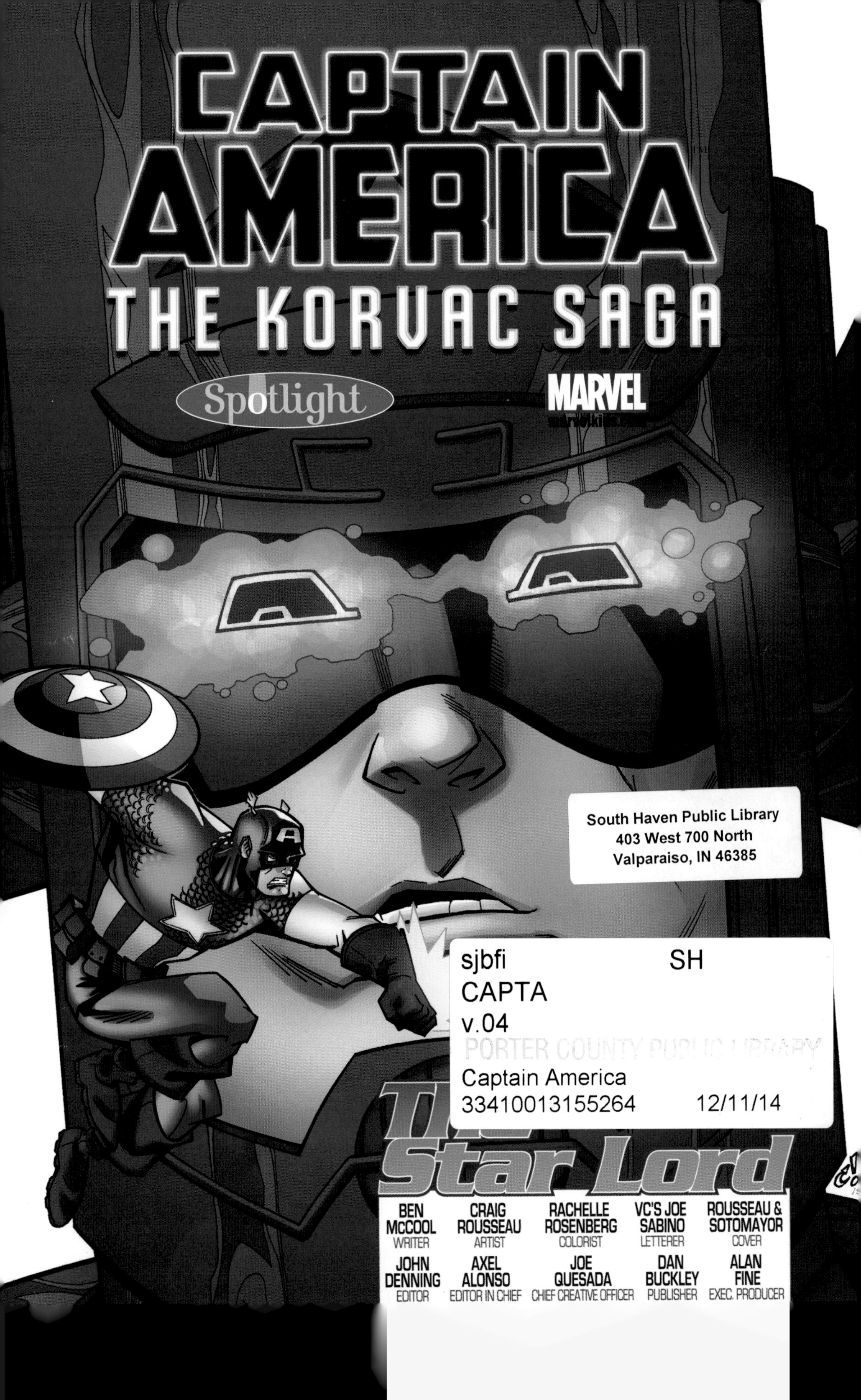
CAPTAIN AMERICA
THE KORVAC SAGA
Spotlight
MARVEL
The Star Lord
BEN McCOOL WRITER
CRAIG ROUSSEAU ARTIST
RACHELLE ROSENBERG COLORIST
VC'S JOE SABINO LETTERER
ROUSSEAU & SOTOMAYOR COVER
JOHN DENNING EDITOR
AXEL ALONSO EDITOR IN CHIEF
JOE QUESADA CHIEF CREATIVE OFFICER
DAN BUCKLEY PUBLISHER
ALAN FINE EXEC. PRODUCER

visit us at www.abdopublishing.com

Reinforced library bound edition published in 2013 by Spotlight, a division of the ABDO Group, PO Box 398166, Minneapolis, MN 55439. Spotlight produces high-quality reinforced library bound editions for schools and libraries. Published by agreement with Marvel Entertainment, LLC. The stories, characters, and incidents mentioned are entirely fictional. All rights reserved. Used under authorization.

Printed in the United States of America, North Mankato, Minnesota.
052012
092012
♻This book contains at least 10% recycled materials.

TM & © 2012 Marvel & Subs.

Library of Congress Cataloging-in-Publication Data

McCool, Ben.
  Captain America : the Korvac saga / story by Ben McCool ; art by Craig Rousseau. -- Reinforced library bound ed.
     <v. 1-> cm.
  "Marvel."
  Summary: Captain America, a proud member of the Avengers, is still trying to find his way in a strange new world when he discovers his connection to a mysterious man named Korvac, who claims to be similarly displaced in time.
  Contents: [v. 1]. Strange days --
  ISBN 978-1-61479-019-8 (Strange days: #1 : alk. paper) -- ISBN 978-1-61479-020-4 (Souljacker: #2 : alk. paper) -- ISBN 978-1-61479-021-1 (The traveler: #3 : alk. paper) -- ISBN 978-1-61479-022-8 (The star lord: #4 : alk. paper)
  1. Graphic novels. [1. Graphic novels. 2. Superheroes--Fiction. 3. Space and time--Fiction.] I. Rousseau, Craig, ill. II. Title.
  PZ7.7.M415Cap 2012
  741.5'973--dc23
                                2012000931
ISBN 978-1-61479-022-8 (reinforced library edition)

All Spotlight books are reinforced library binding
and manufactured in the United States of America.

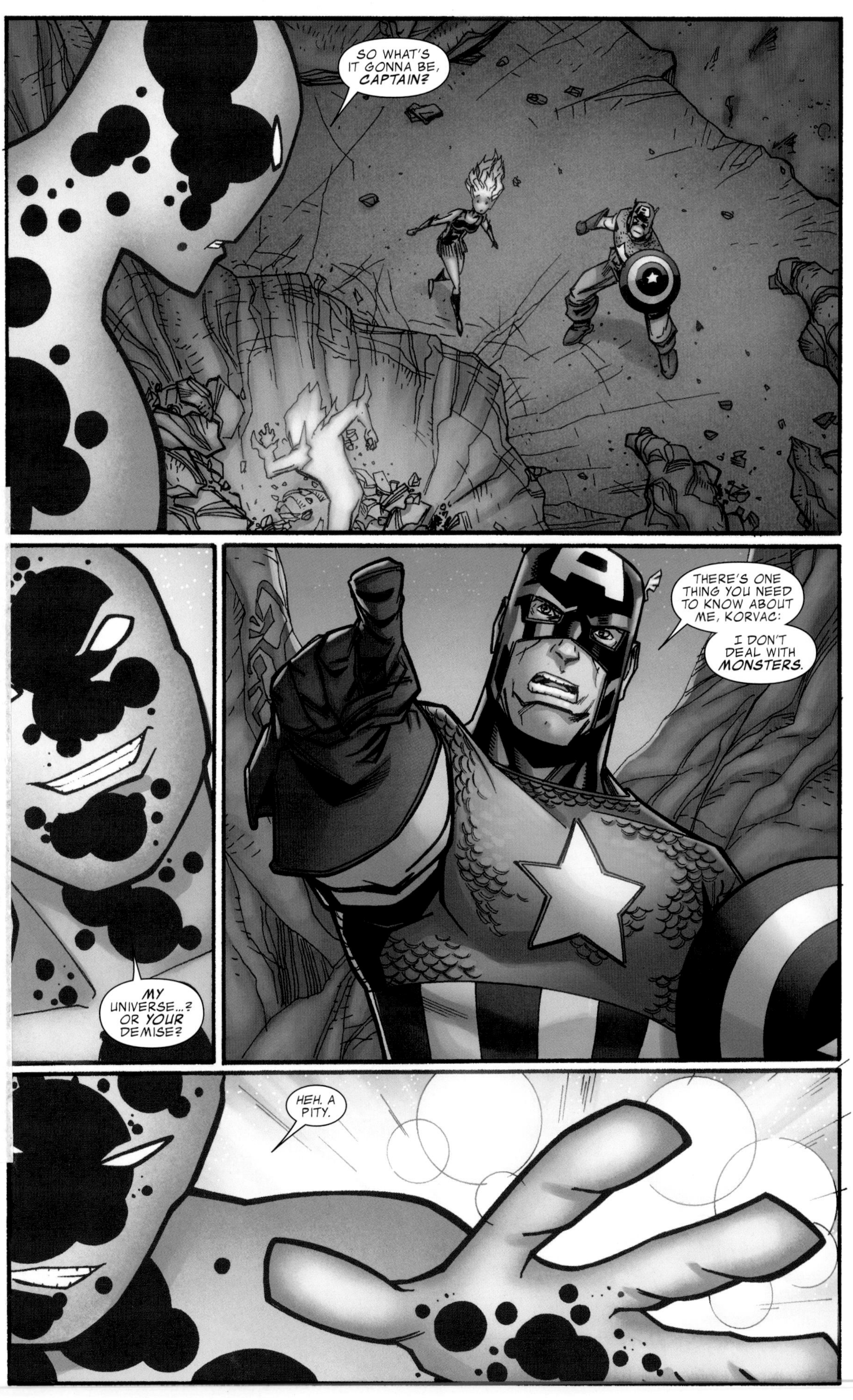
SO WHAT'S IT GONNA BE, CAPTAIN?
MY UNIVERSE...? OR YOUR DEMISE?
THERE'S ONE THING YOU NEED TO KNOW ABOUT ME, KORVAC:
I DON'T DEAL WITH MONSTERS.
HEH. A PITY.

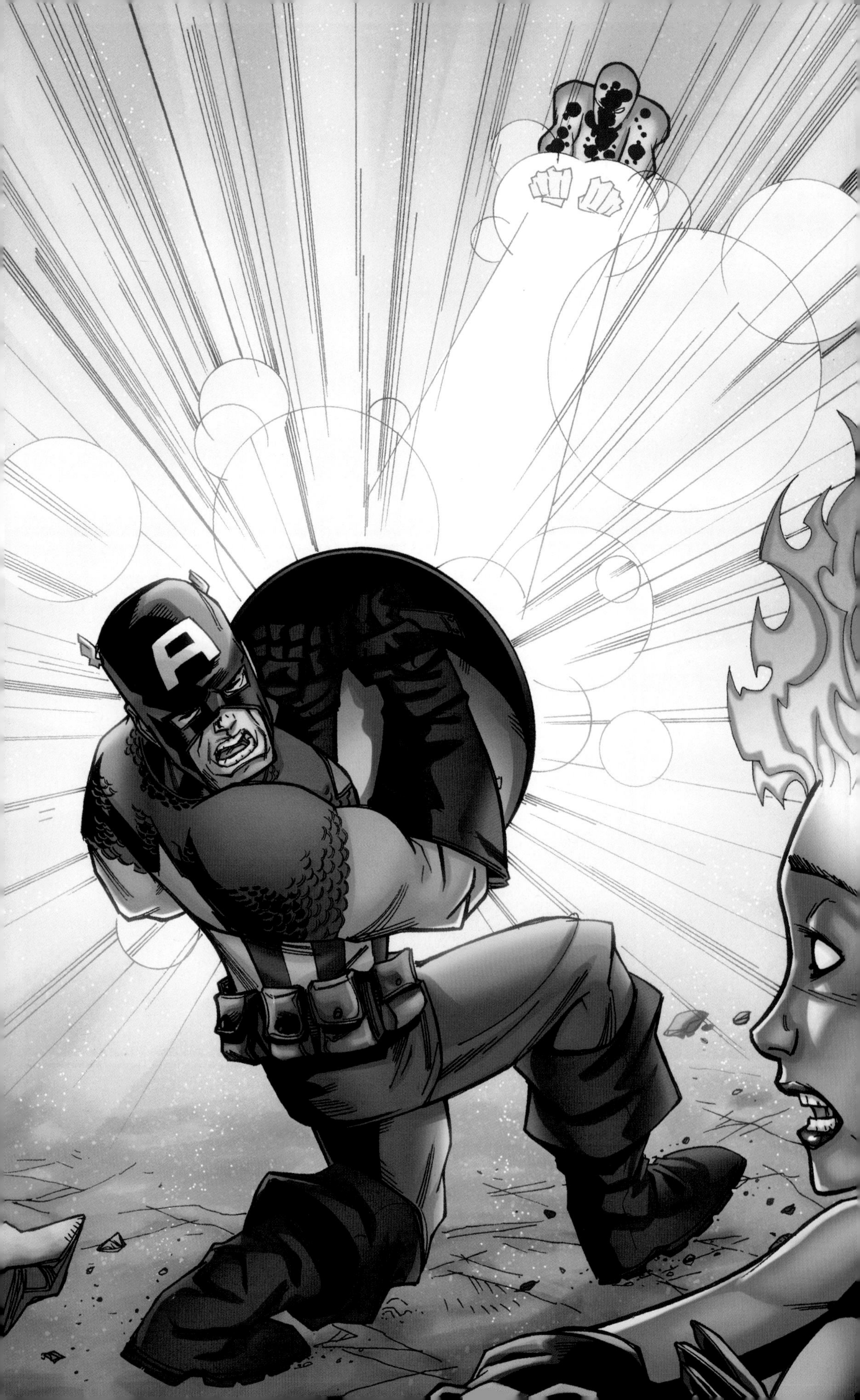

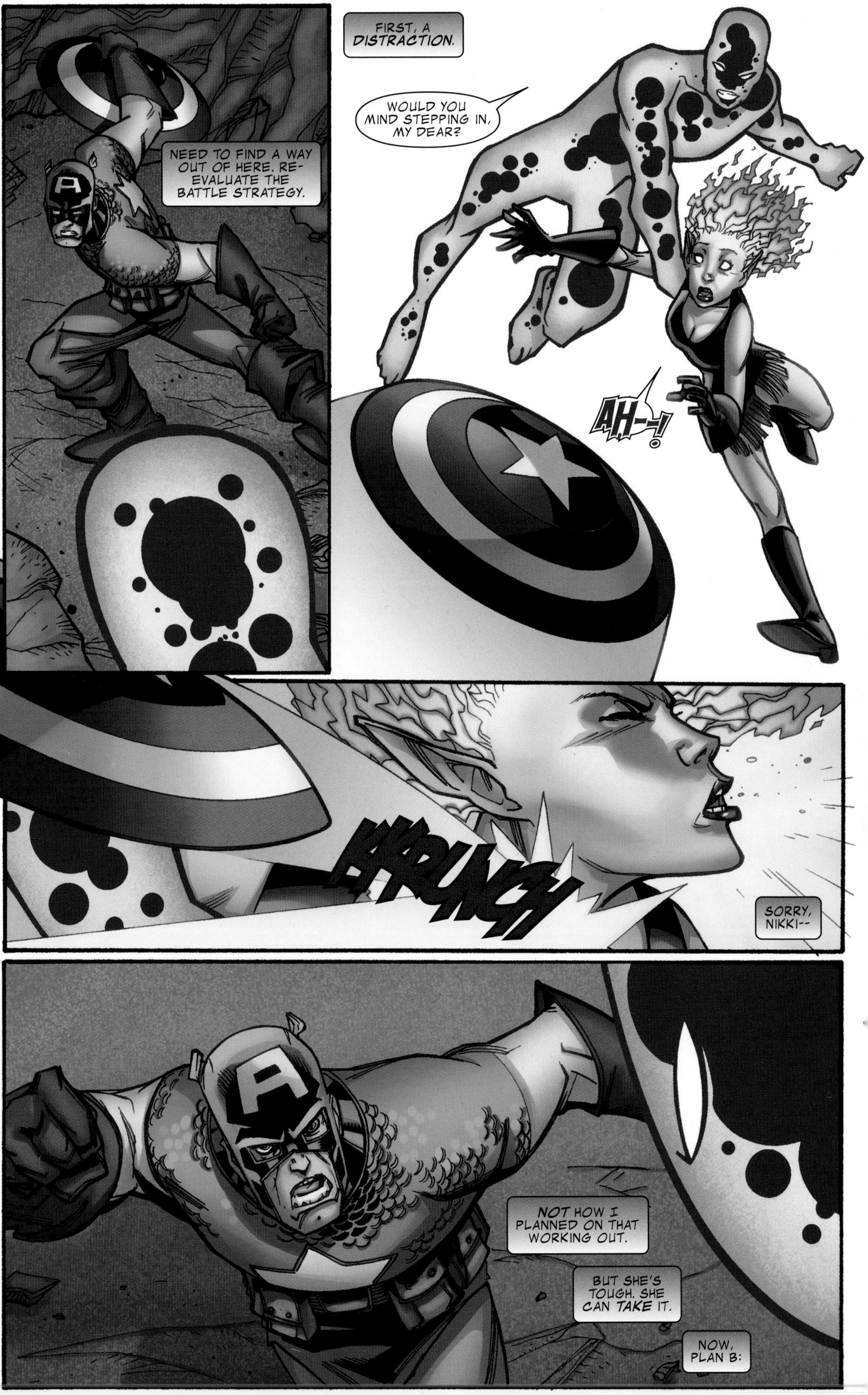
NEED TO FIND A WAY OUT OF HERE. RE-EVALUATE THE BATTLE STRATEGY.
FIRST, A DISTRACTION.
WOULD YOU MIND STEPPING IN, MY DEAR?
AH--!
KRUNCH
SORRY, NIKKI--
NOT HOW I PLANNED ON THAT WORKING OUT.
BUT SHE'S TOUGH. SHE CAN TAKE IT.
NOW, PLAN B:

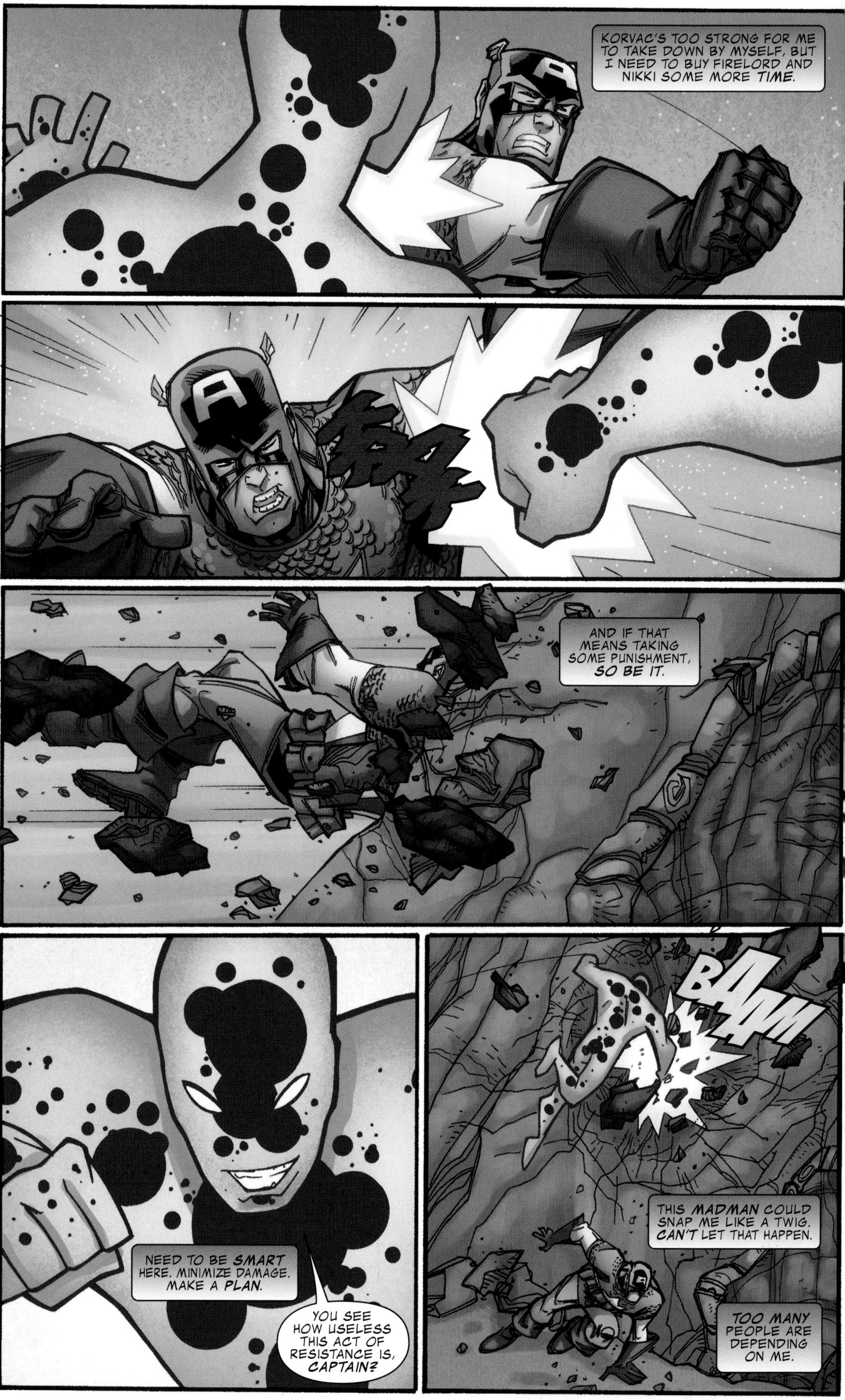
KORVAC'S TOO STRONG FOR ME TO TAKE DOWN BY MYSELF, BUT I NEED TO BUY FIRELORD AND NIKKI SOME MORE *TIME*.
AND IF THAT MEANS TAKING SOME PUNISHMENT, **SO BE IT**.
NEED TO BE *SMART* HERE. MINIMIZE DAMAGE. MAKE A *PLAN*.
YOU SEE HOW USELESS THIS ACT OF RESISTANCE IS, **CAPTAIN?**
THIS *MADMAN* COULD SNAP ME LIKE A TWIG. *CAN'T* LET THAT HAPPEN.
TOO MANY PEOPLE ARE DEPENDING ON ME.

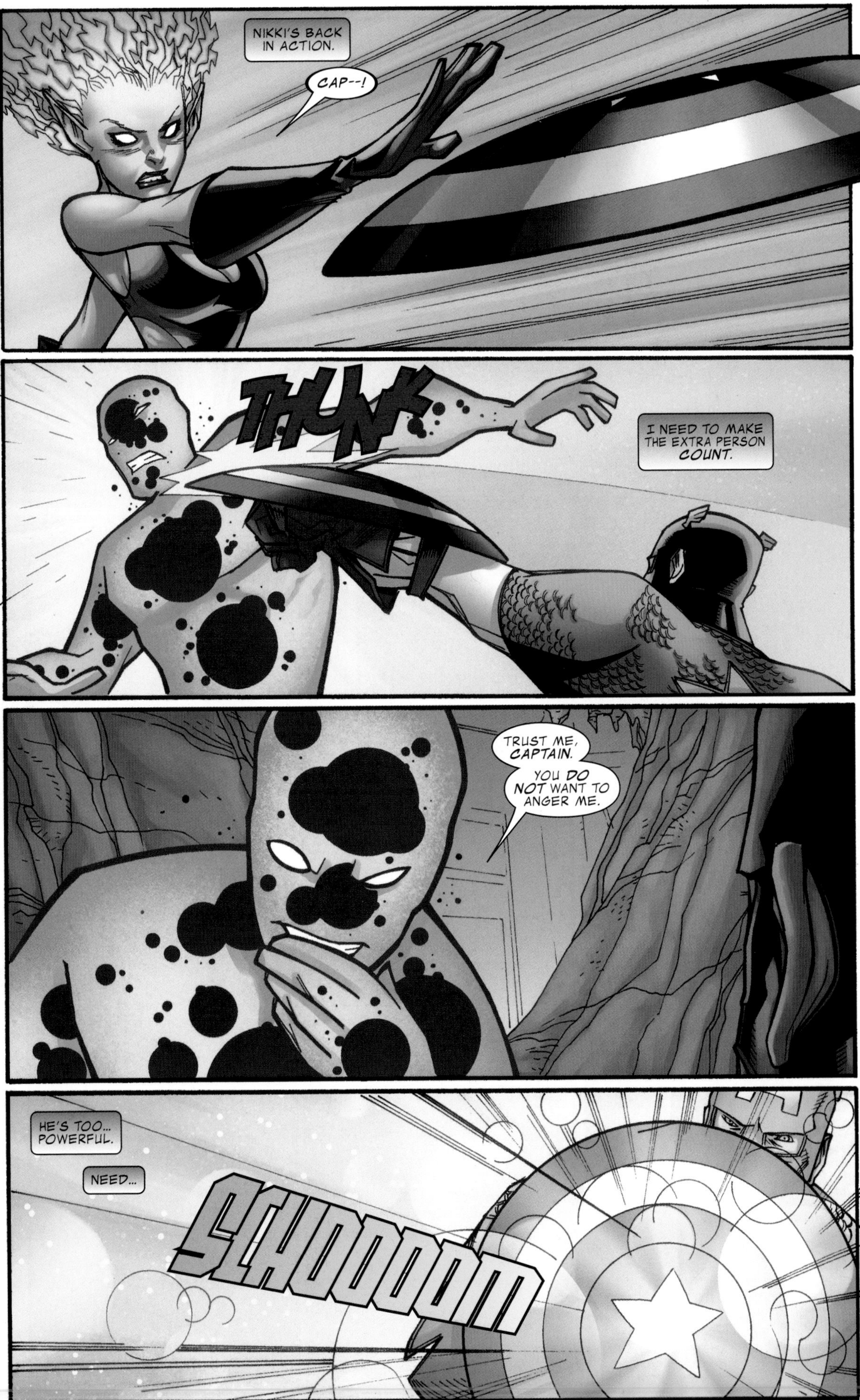
NIKKI'S BACK IN ACTION.
CAP--!
THUNK
I NEED TO MAKE THE EXTRA PERSON COUNT.
TRUST ME, CAPTAIN.
YOU DO NOT WANT TO ANGER ME.
HE'S TOO... POWERFUL.
NEED...
SCHOOOOM

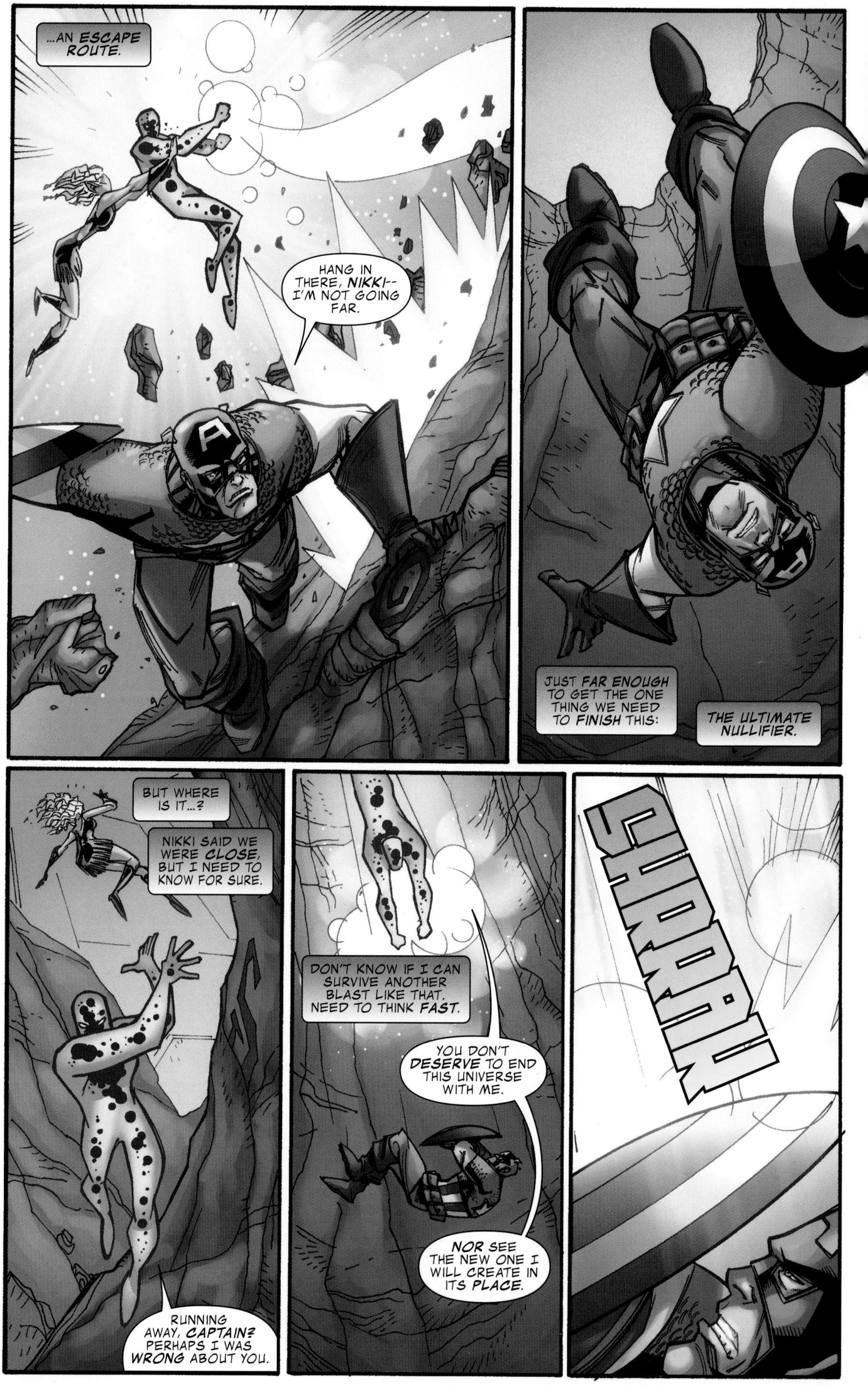
...AN ESCAPE ROUTE.
HANG IN THERE, NIKKI-- I'M NOT GOING FAR.
JUST FAR ENOUGH TO GET THE ONE THING WE NEED TO FINISH THIS:
THE ULTIMATE NULLIFIER.
BUT WHERE IS IT...?
NIKKI SAID WE WERE CLOSE, BUT I NEED TO KNOW FOR SURE.
RUNNING AWAY, CAPTAIN? PERHAPS I WAS WRONG ABOUT YOU.
DON'T KNOW IF I CAN SURVIVE ANOTHER BLAST LIKE THAT. NEED TO THINK FAST.
YOU DON'T DESERVE TO END THIS UNIVERSE WITH ME.
NOR SEE THE NEW ONE I WILL CREATE IN ITS PLACE.
SHRRAK

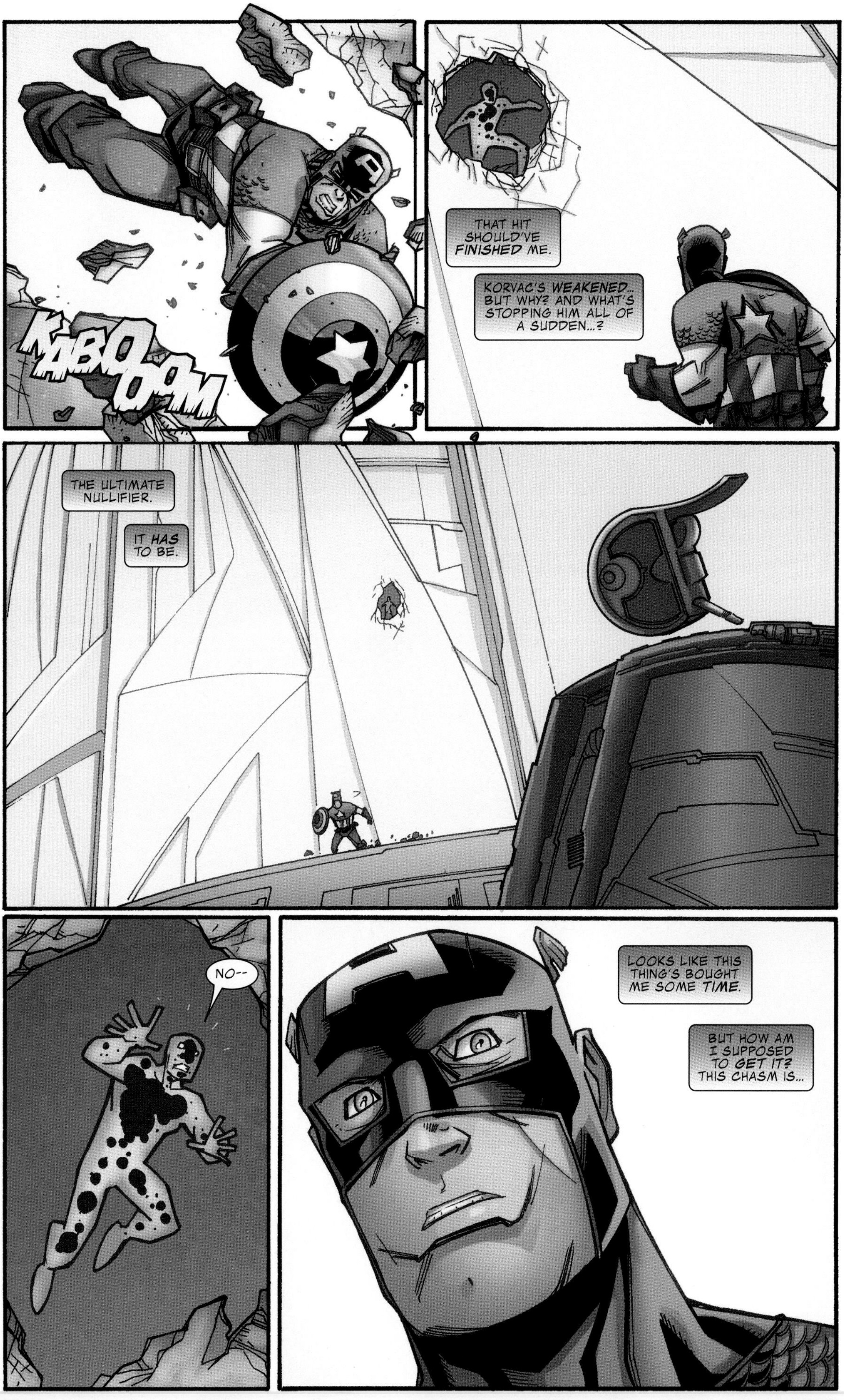
KABOOOOM
THAT HIT SHOULD'VE FINISHED ME.
KORVAC'S WEAKENED... BUT WHY? AND WHAT'S STOPPING HIM ALL OF A SUDDEN...?
THE ULTIMATE NULLIFIER.
IT HAS TO BE.
NO--
LOOKS LIKE THIS THING'S BOUGHT ME SOME TIME.
BUT HOW AM I SUPPOSED TO GET IT? THIS CHASM IS...

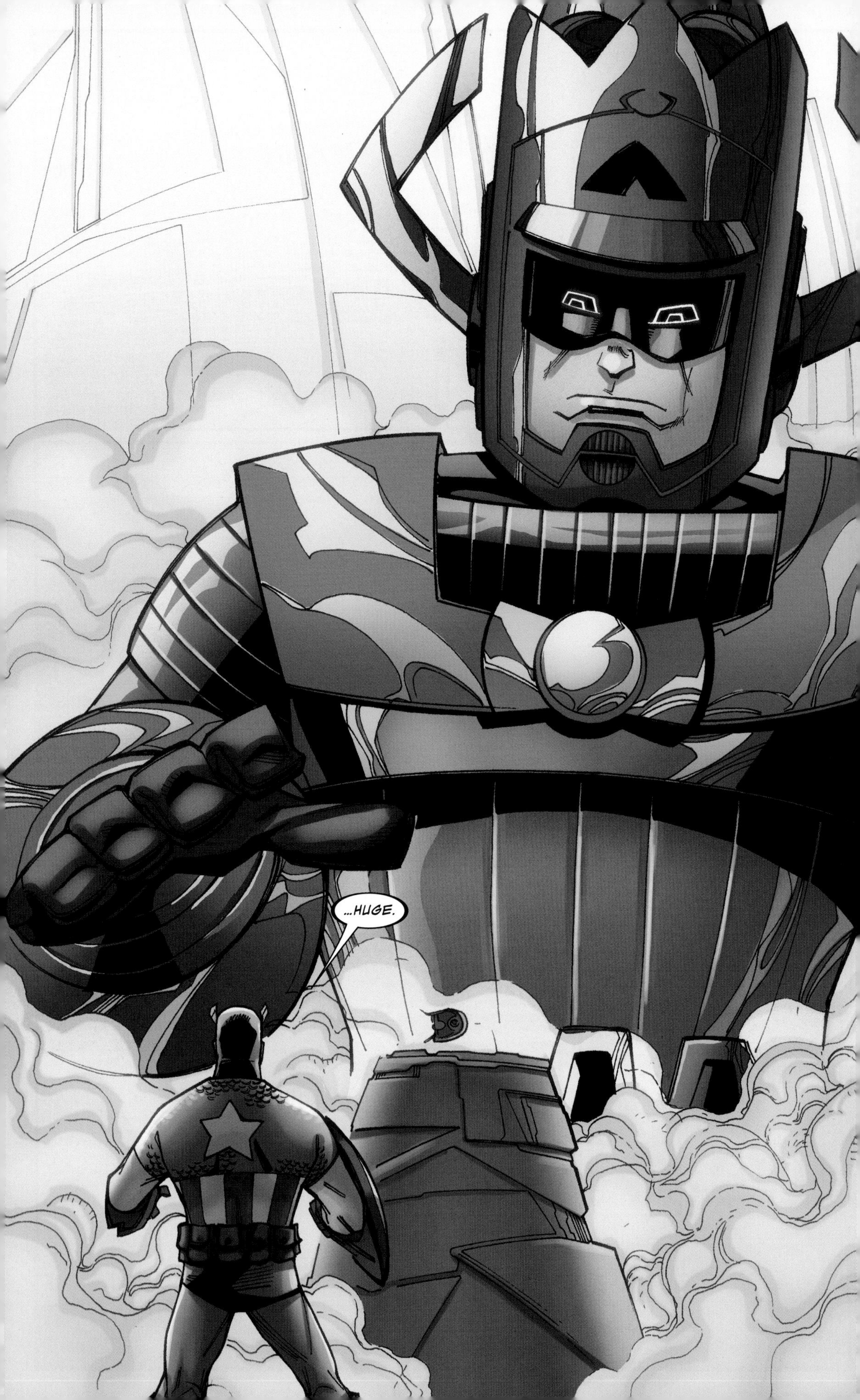
...HUGE.

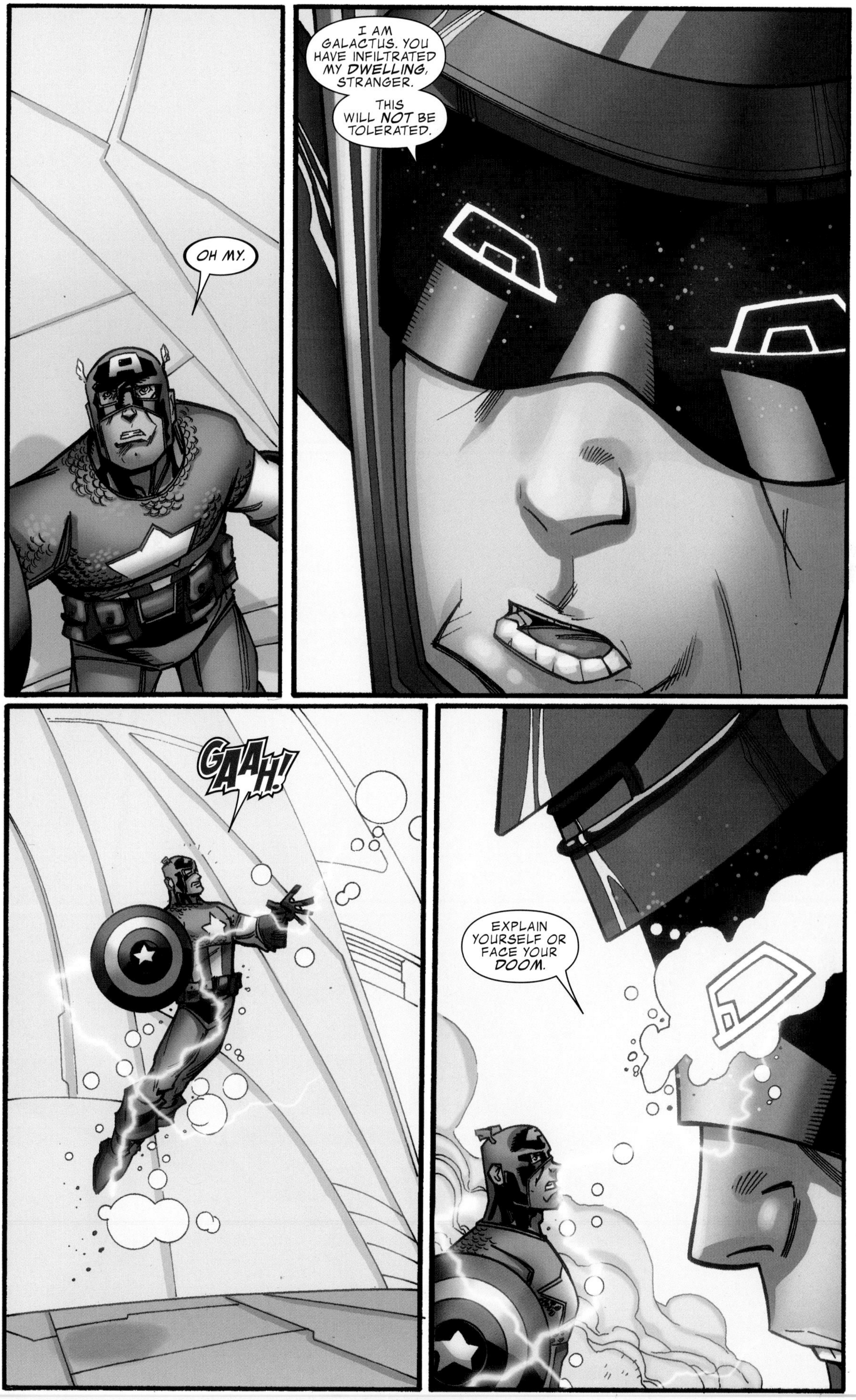
OH MY.
I AM GALACTUS. YOU HAVE INFILTRATED MY DWELLING, STRANGER.
THIS WILL NOT BE TOLERATED.
GAAH!
EXPLAIN YOURSELF OR FACE YOUR DOOM.

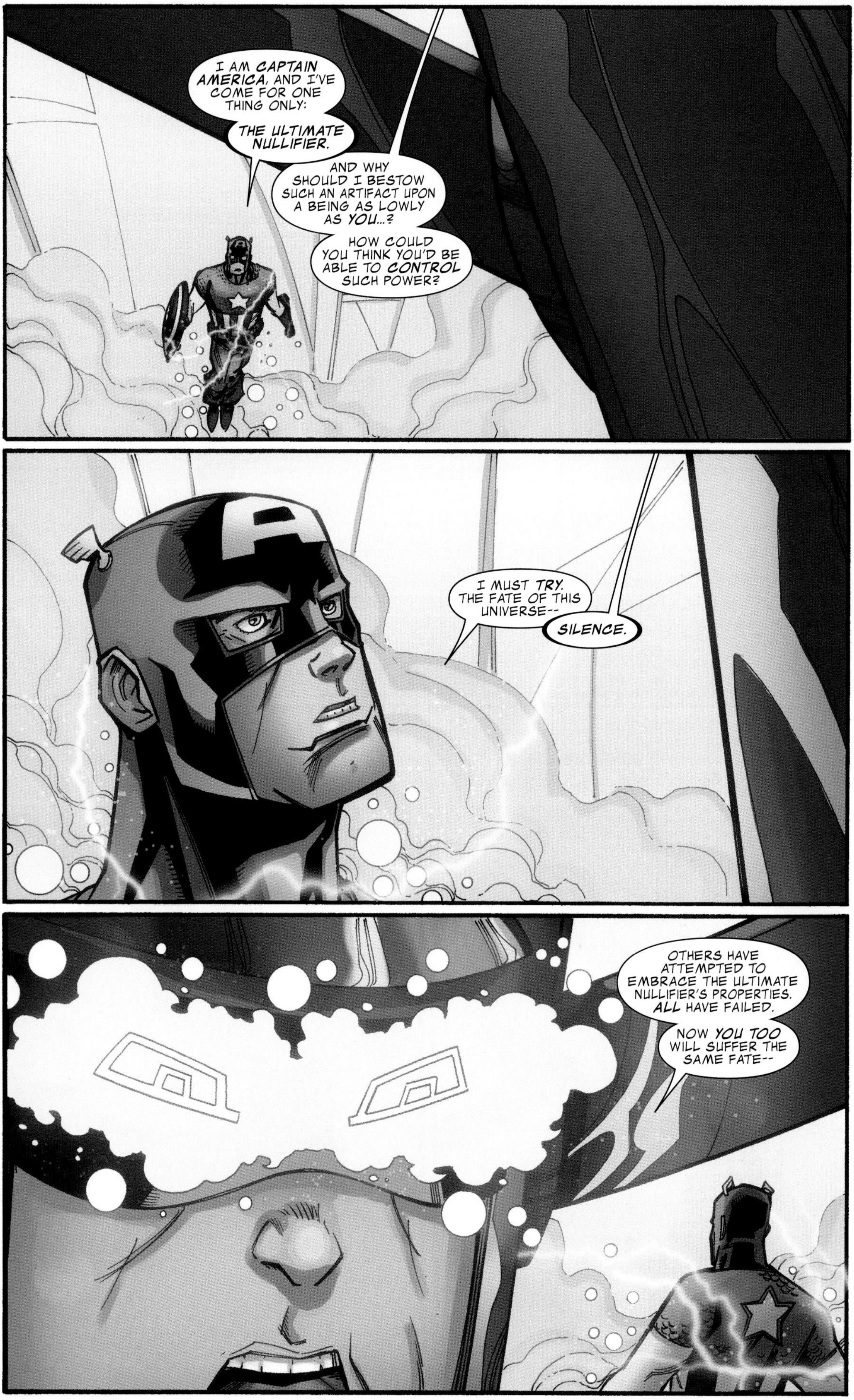
I AM CAPTAIN AMERICA, AND I'VE COME FOR ONE THING ONLY:
THE ULTIMATE NULLIFIER.
AND WHY SHOULD I BESTOW SUCH AN ARTIFACT UPON A BEING AS LOWLY AS YOU...?
HOW COULD YOU THINK YOU'D BE ABLE TO CONTROL SUCH POWER?
I MUST TRY. THE FATE OF THIS UNIVERSE--
SILENCE.
OTHERS HAVE ATTEMPTED TO EMBRACE THE ULTIMATE NULLIFIER'S PROPERTIES. ALL HAVE FAILED.
NOW YOU TOO WILL SUFFER THE SAME FATE--

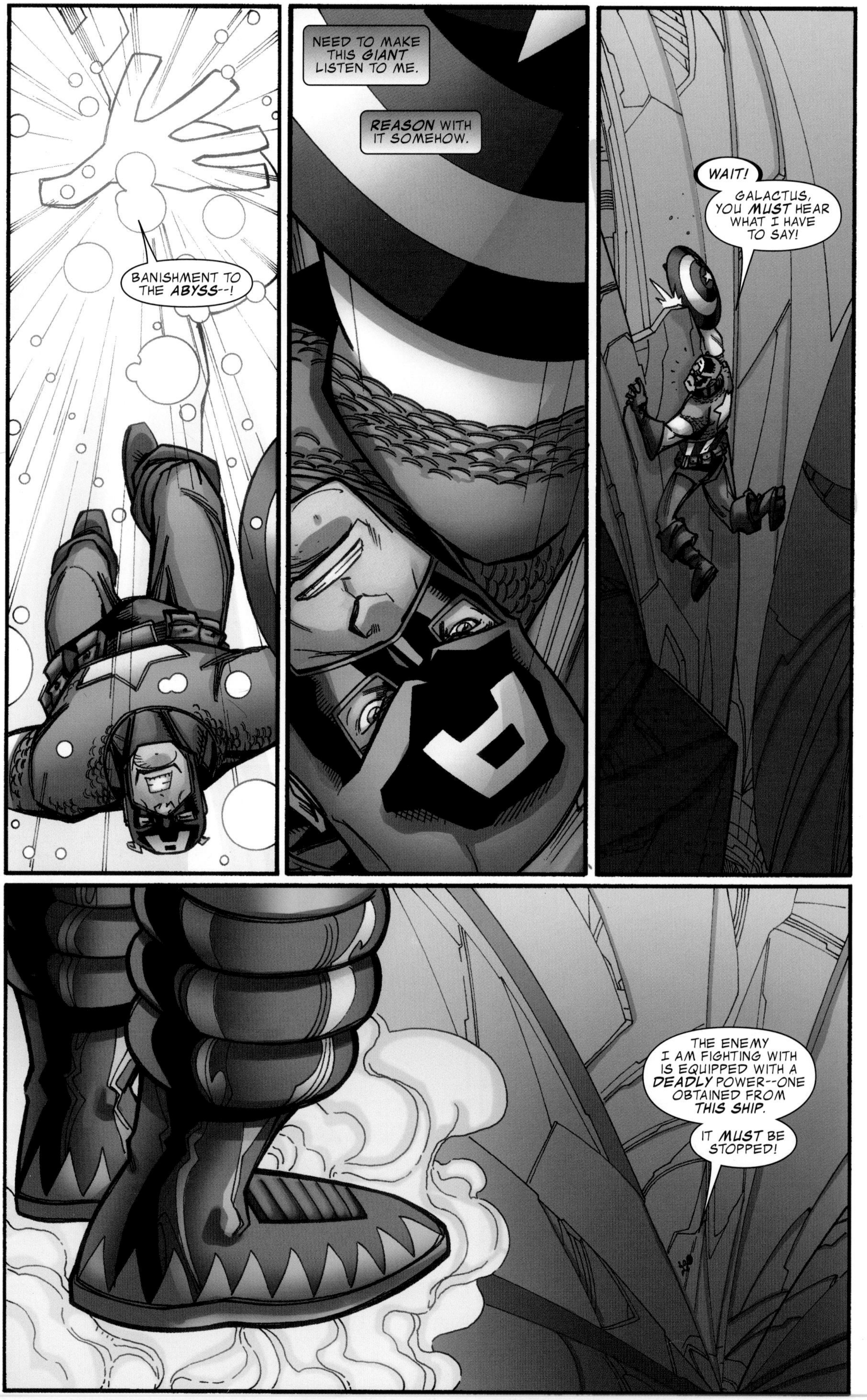
BANISHMENT TO THE ABYSS--!
NEED TO MAKE THIS GIANT LISTEN TO ME.
REASON WITH IT SOMEHOW.
WAIT!
GALACTUS, YOU MUST HEAR WHAT I HAVE TO SAY!
THE ENEMY I AM FIGHTING WITH IS EQUIPPED WITH A DEADLY POWER--ONE OBTAINED FROM THIS SHIP.
IT MUST BE STOPPED!

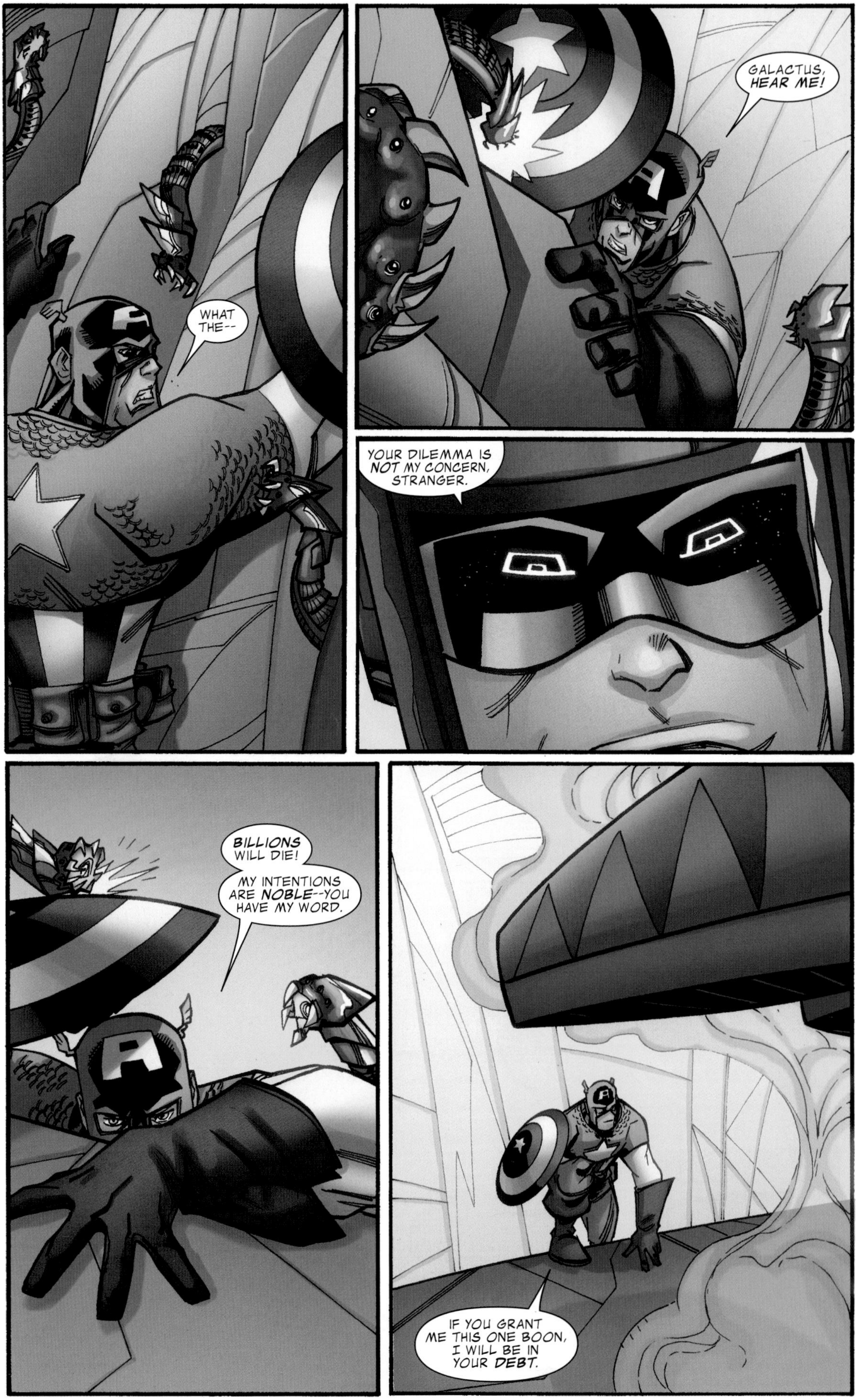
WHAT THE--
GALACTUS, HEAR ME!
YOUR DILEMMA IS NOT MY CONCERN, STRANGER.
BILLIONS WILL DIE!
MY INTENTIONS ARE NOBLE--YOU HAVE MY WORD.
IF YOU GRANT ME THIS ONE BOON, I WILL BE IN YOUR DEBT.

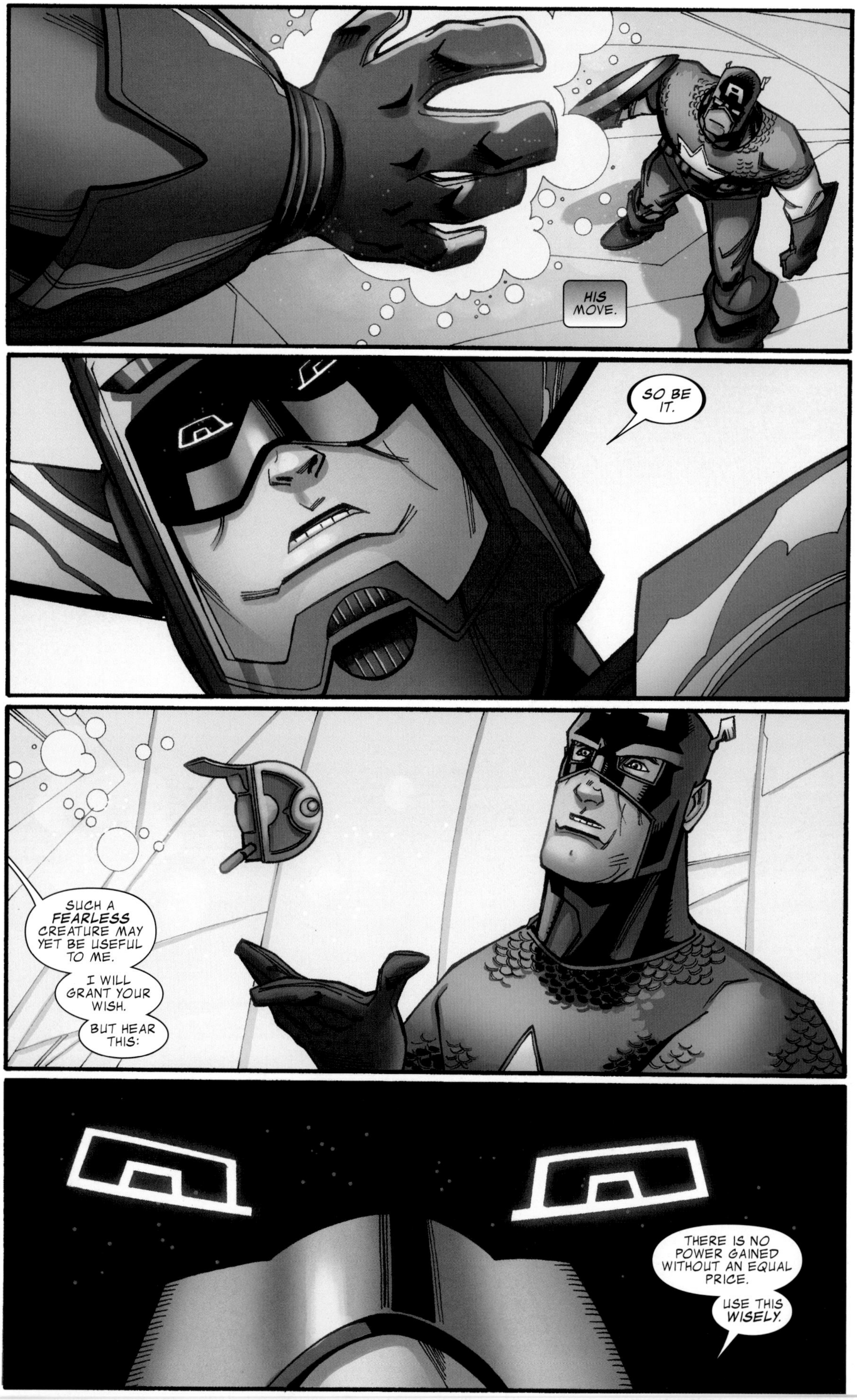
HIS MOVE.
SO BE IT.
SUCH A FEARLESS CREATURE MAY YET BE USEFUL TO ME.
I WILL GRANT YOUR WISH.
BUT HEAR THIS:
THERE IS NO POWER GAINED WITHOUT AN EQUAL PRICE.
USE THIS WISELY.

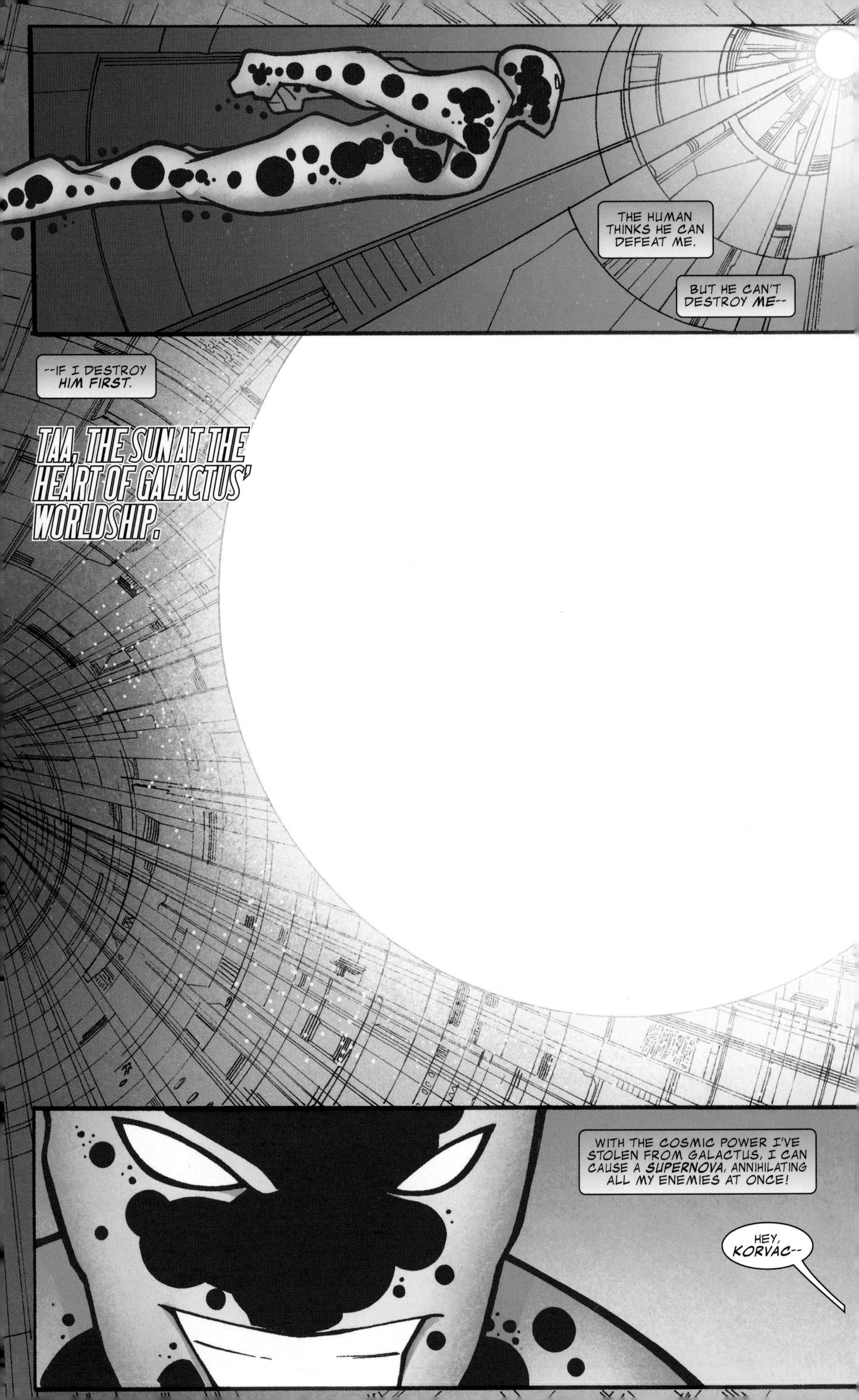
THE HUMAN THINKS HE CAN DEFEAT ME.
BUT HE CAN'T DESTROY ME--
--IF I DESTROY HIM FIRST.
TAA, THE SUN AT THE HEART OF GALACTUS' WORLDSHIP.
WITH THE COSMIC POWER I'VE STOLEN FROM GALACTUS, I CAN CAUSE A SUPERNOVA, ANNIHILATING ALL MY ENEMIES AT ONCE!
HEY, KORVAC--

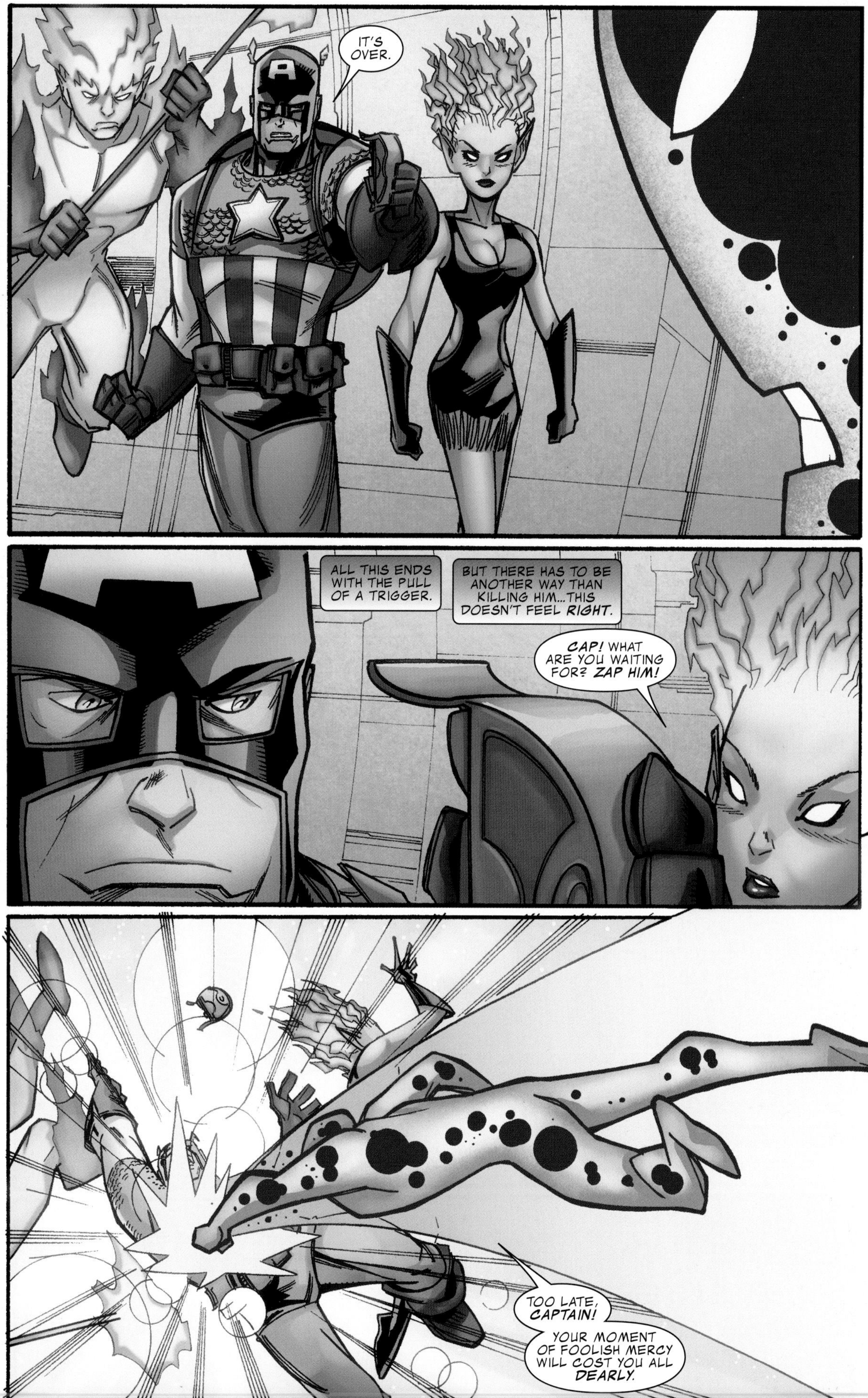
IT'S OVER.
ALL THIS ENDS WITH THE PULL OF A TRIGGER.
BUT THERE HAS TO BE ANOTHER WAY THAN KILLING HIM...THIS DOESN'T FEEL RIGHT.
CAP! WHAT ARE YOU WAITING FOR? ZAP HIM!
TOO LATE, CAPTAIN!
YOUR MOMENT OF FOOLISH MERCY WILL COST YOU ALL DEARLY.

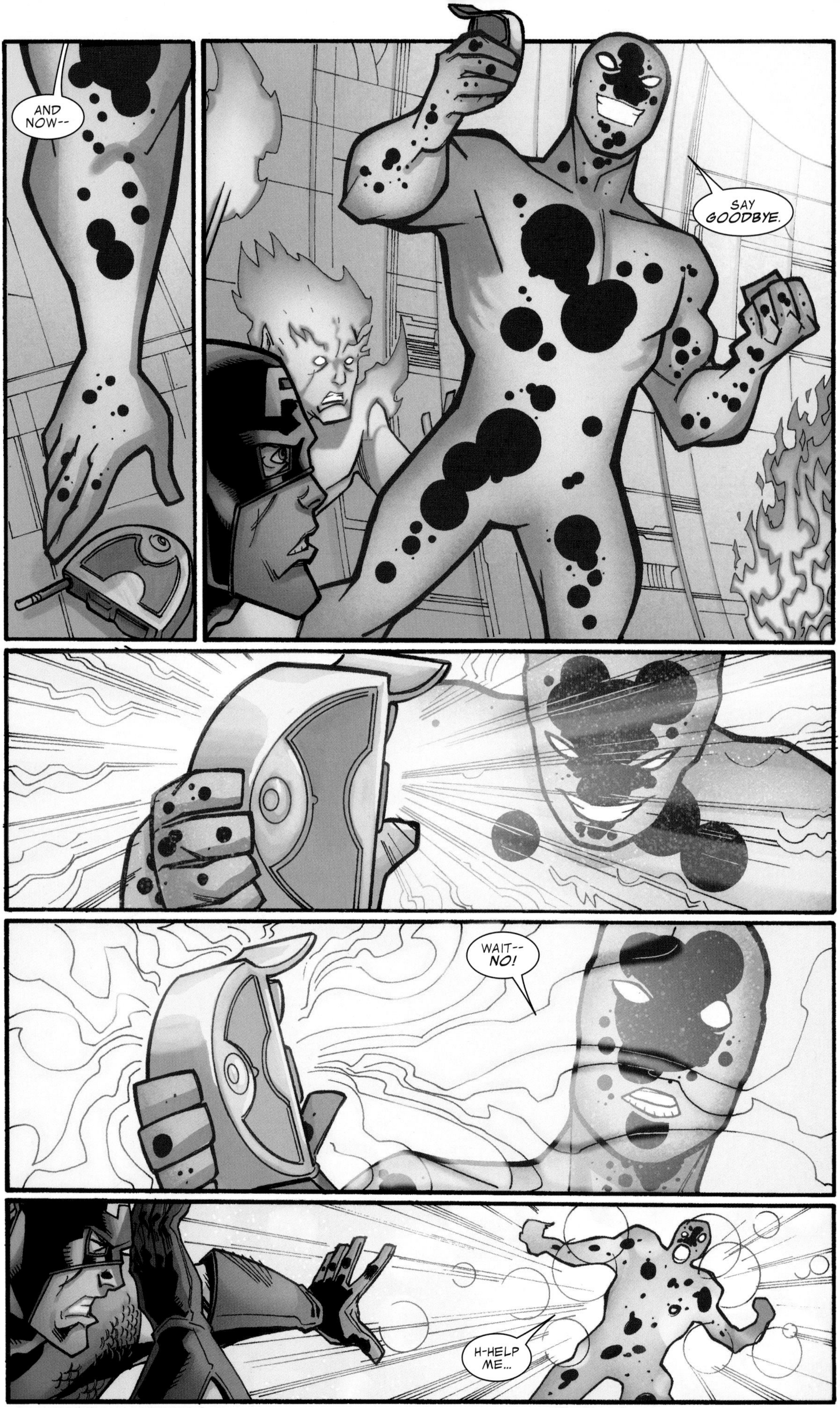
AND NOW--
SAY GOODBYE.
WAIT-- NO!
H-HELP ME...

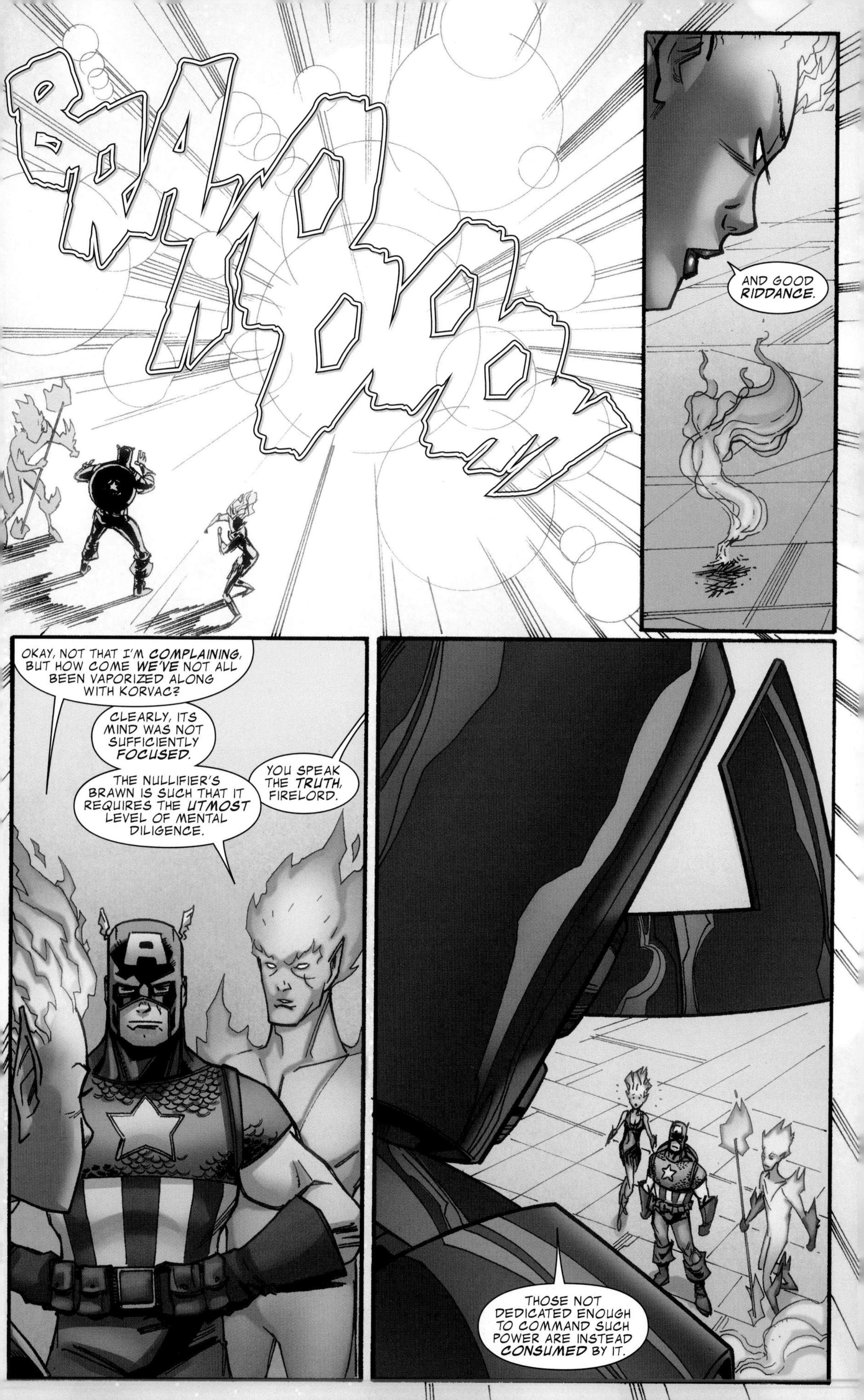
AND GOOD RIDDANCE.
OKAY, NOT THAT I'M COMPLAINING, BUT HOW COME WE'VE NOT ALL BEEN VAPORIZED ALONG WITH KORVAC?
CLEARLY, ITS MIND WAS NOT SUFFICIENTLY FOCUSED.
THE NULLIFIER'S BRAWN IS SUCH THAT IT REQUIRES THE UTMOST LEVEL OF MENTAL DILIGENCE.
YOU SPEAK THE TRUTH, FIRELORD.
THOSE NOT DEDICATED ENOUGH TO COMMAND SUCH POWER ARE INSTEAD CONSUMED BY IT.

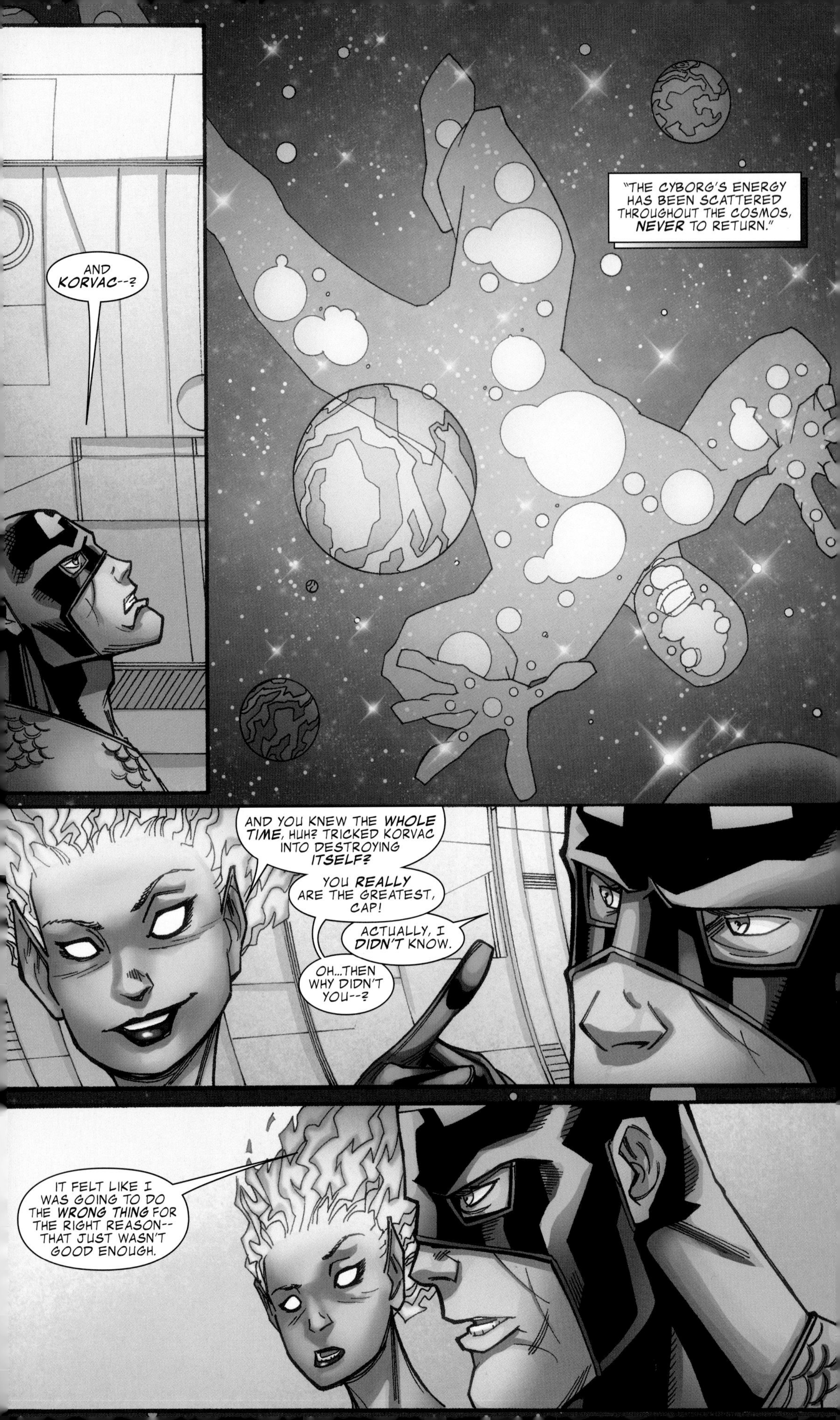
AND KORVAC--?
"THE CYBORG'S ENERGY HAS BEEN SCATTERED THROUGHOUT THE COSMOS, NEVER TO RETURN."
AND YOU KNEW THE WHOLE TIME, HUH? TRICKED KORVAC INTO DESTROYING ITSELF?
YOU REALLY ARE THE GREATEST, CAP!
ACTUALLY, I DIDN'T KNOW.
OH...THEN WHY DIDN'T YOU--?
IT FELT LIKE I WAS GOING TO DO THE WRONG THING FOR THE RIGHT REASON-- THAT JUST WASN'T GOOD ENOUGH.

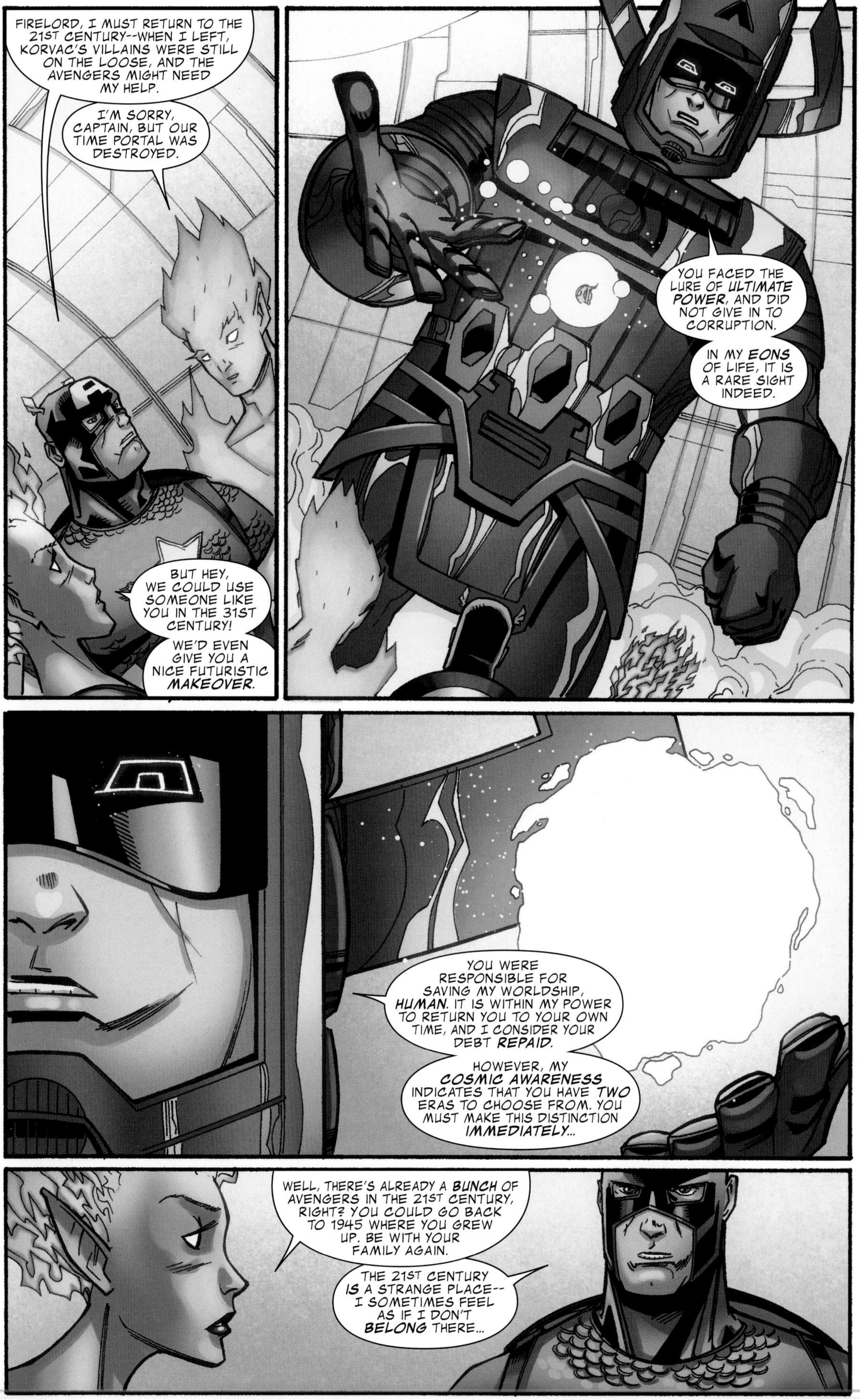
FIRELORD, I MUST RETURN TO THE 21ST CENTURY--WHEN I LEFT, KORVAC'S VILLAINS WERE STILL ON THE LOOSE, AND THE AVENGERS MIGHT NEED MY HELP.
I'M SORRY, CAPTAIN, BUT OUR TIME PORTAL WAS DESTROYED.
BUT HEY, WE COULD USE SOMEONE LIKE YOU IN THE 31ST CENTURY!
WE'D EVEN GIVE YOU A NICE FUTURISTIC MAKEOVER.
YOU FACED THE LURE OF ULTIMATE POWER, AND DID NOT GIVE IN TO CORRUPTION.
IN MY EONS OF LIFE, IT IS A RARE SIGHT INDEED.
YOU WERE RESPONSIBLE FOR SAVING MY WORLDSHIP, HUMAN. IT IS WITHIN MY POWER TO RETURN YOU TO YOUR OWN TIME, AND I CONSIDER YOUR DEBT REPAID.
HOWEVER, MY COSMIC AWARENESS INDICATES THAT YOU HAVE TWO ERAS TO CHOOSE FROM. YOU MUST MAKE THIS DISTINCTION IMMEDIATELY...
WELL, THERE'S ALREADY A BUNCH OF AVENGERS IN THE 21ST CENTURY, RIGHT? YOU COULD GO BACK TO 1945 WHERE YOU GREW UP. BE WITH YOUR FAMILY AGAIN.
THE 21ST CENTURY IS A STRANGE PLACE-- I SOMETIMES FEEL AS IF I DON'T BELONG THERE...

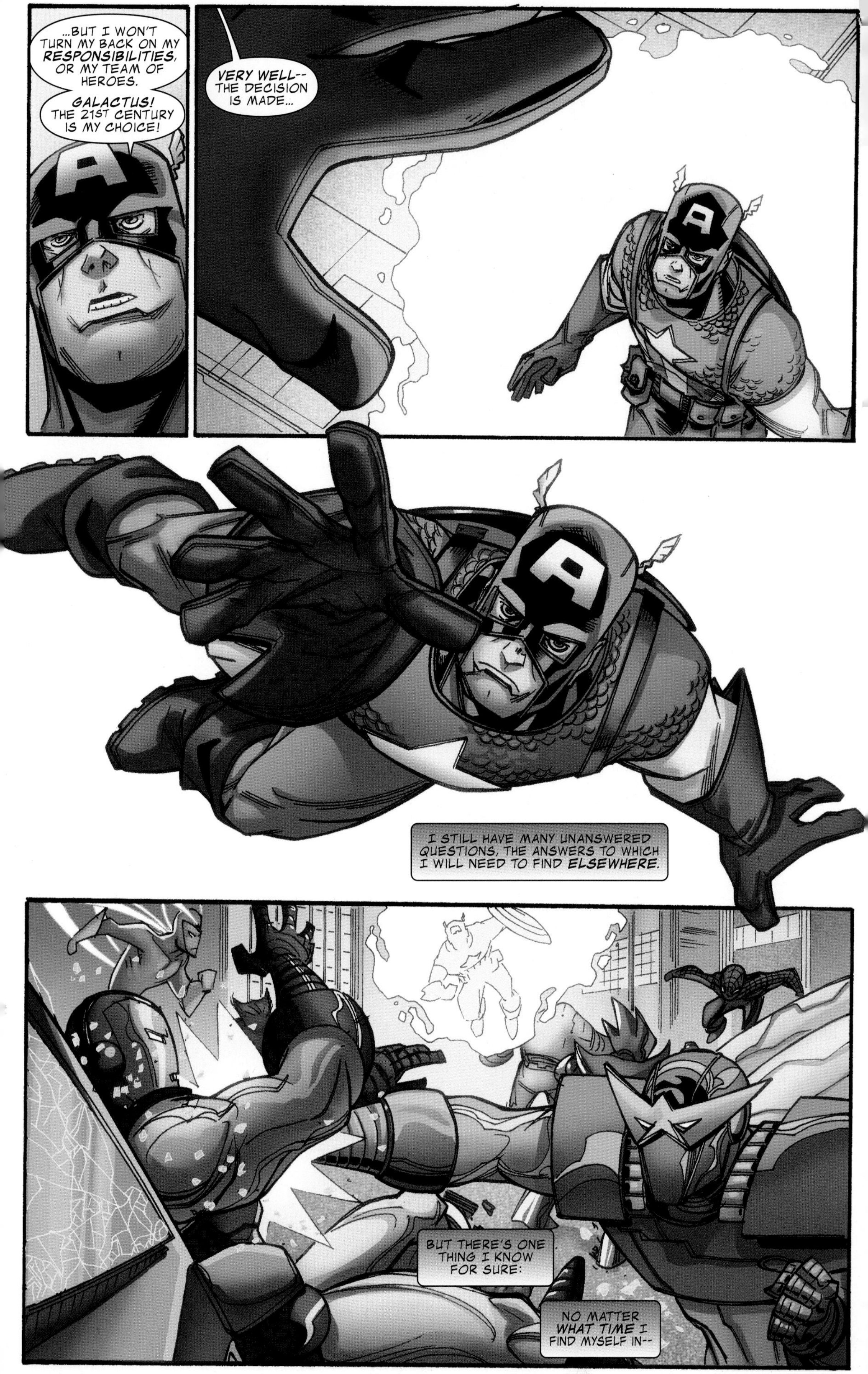

...BUT I WON'T TURN MY BACK ON MY RESPONSIBILITIES, OR MY TEAM OF HEROES.
GALACTUS! THE 21ST CENTURY IS MY CHOICE!
VERY WELL-- THE DECISION IS MADE...
I STILL HAVE MANY UNANSWERED QUESTIONS, THE ANSWERS TO WHICH I WILL NEED TO FIND ELSEWHERE.
BUT THERE'S ONE THING I KNOW FOR SURE:
NO MATTER WHAT TIME I FIND MYSELF IN--

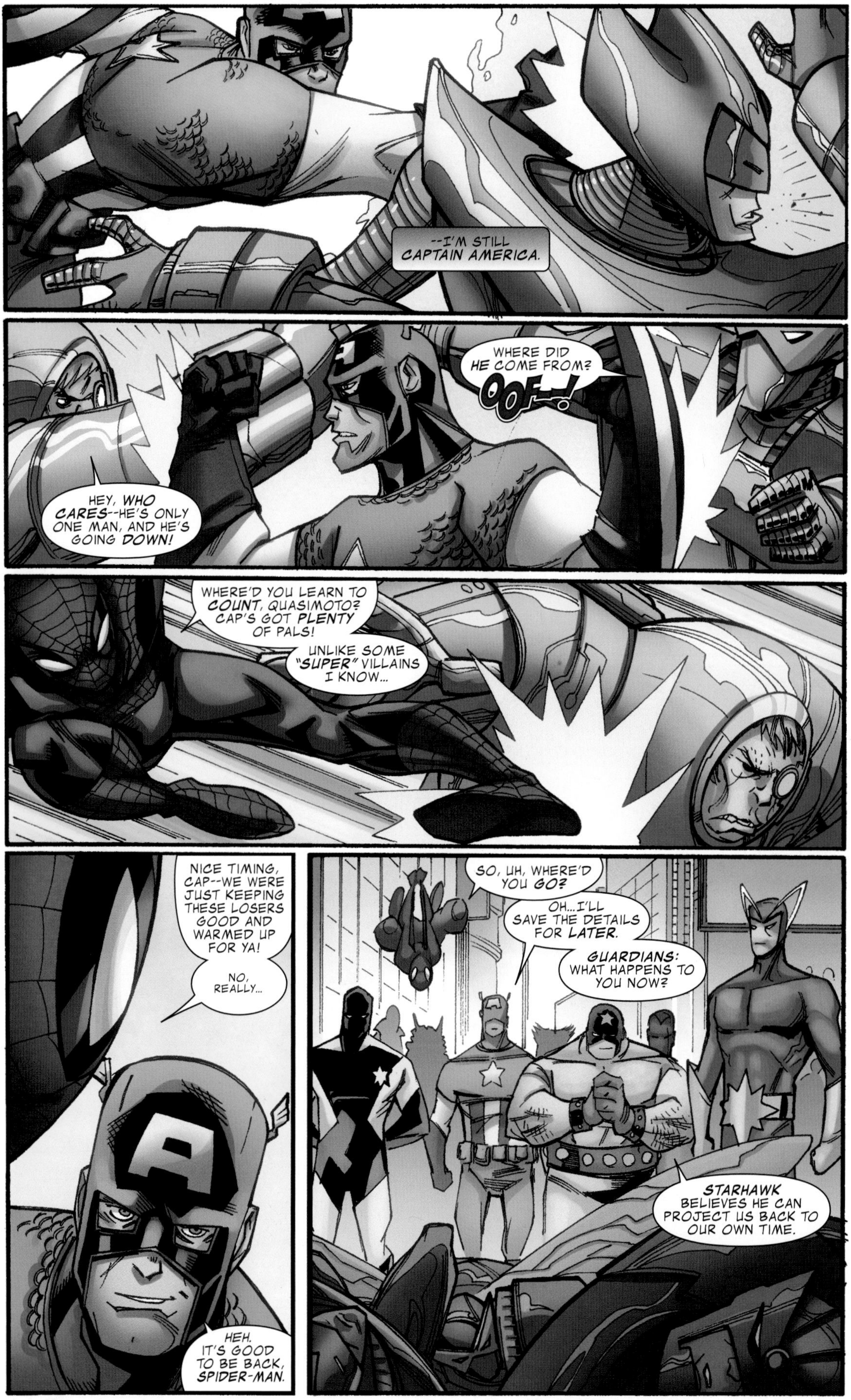
--I'M STILL CAPTAIN AMERICA.
WHERE DID HE COME FROM?
OOF--!
HEY, WHO CARES--HE'S ONLY ONE MAN, AND HE'S GOING DOWN!
WHERE'D YOU LEARN TO COUNT, QUASIMOTO? CAP'S GOT PLENTY OF PALS!
UNLIKE SOME "SUPER" VILLAINS I KNOW...
NICE TIMING, CAP--WE WERE JUST KEEPING THESE LOSERS GOOD AND WARMED UP FOR YA!
NO, REALLY...
HEH. IT'S GOOD TO BE BACK, SPIDER-MAN.
SO, UH, WHERE'D YOU GO?
OH...I'LL SAVE THE DETAILS FOR LATER.
GUARDIANS: WHAT HAPPENS TO YOU NOW?
STARHAWK BELIEVES HE CAN PROJECT US BACK TO OUR OWN TIME.

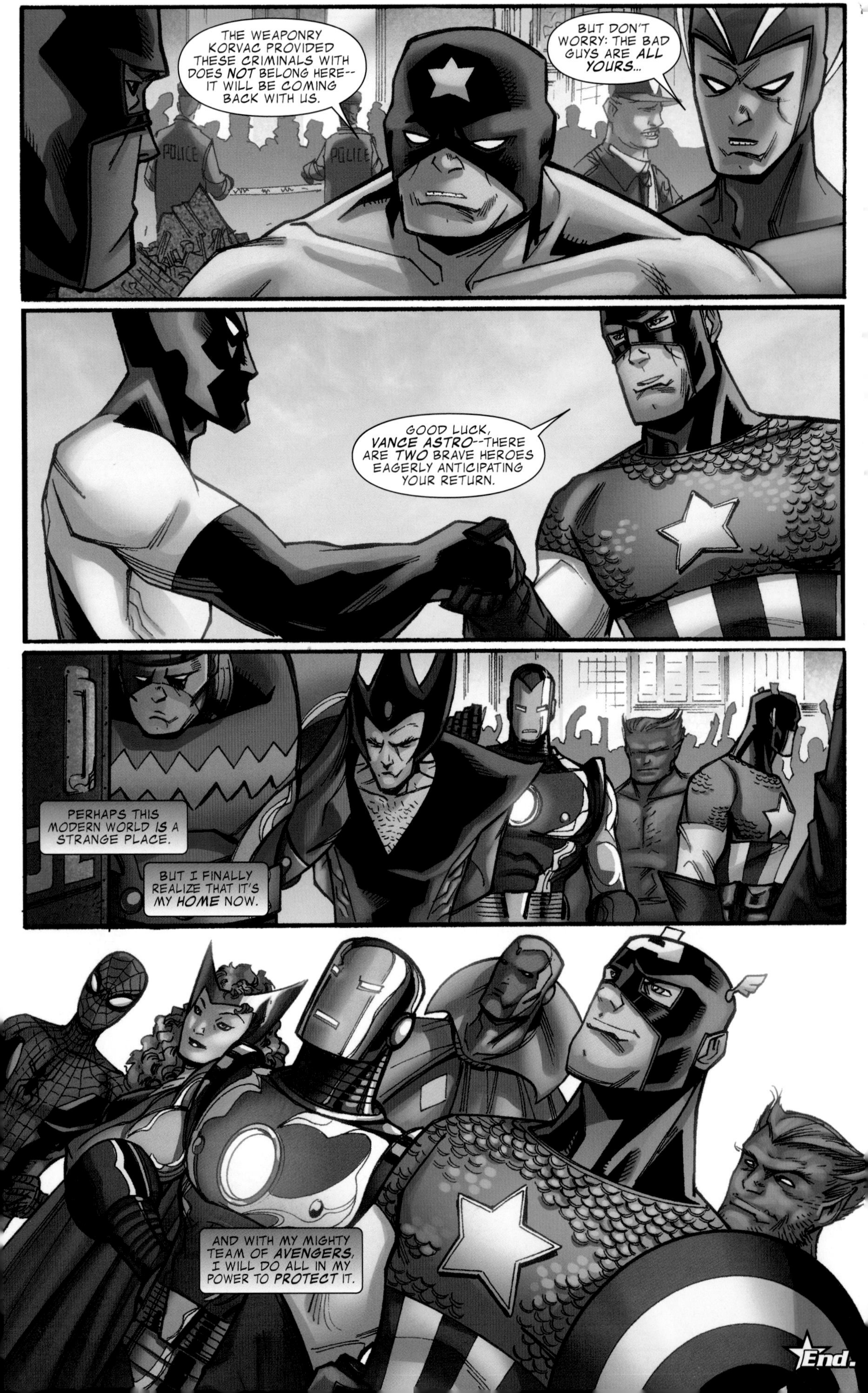
THE WEAPONRY KORVAC PROVIDED THESE CRIMINALS WITH DOES NOT BELONG HERE-- IT WILL BE COMING BACK WITH US.
BUT DON'T WORRY: THE BAD GUYS ARE ALL YOURS...
POLICE
POLICE
GOOD LUCK, VANCE ASTRO--THERE ARE TWO BRAVE HEROES EAGERLY ANTICIPATING YOUR RETURN.
PERHAPS THIS MODERN WORLD IS A STRANGE PLACE.
BUT I FINALLY REALIZE THAT IT'S MY HOME NOW.
AND WITH MY MIGHTY TEAM OF AVENGERS, I WILL DO ALL IN MY POWER TO PROTECT IT.
End.